EX-LIBRIS

Presented by
the Sebastian
Brant Society
in memory of
STAN MARX

MADE UP and
COLORED BY
VLAdIMIR
RAdUNSKY

Edward

An Edward Lear

ALPHABET

HARPERCOLLINSPUBLISHERS

A

A was once an apple pie,
Pidy
Widy
Tidy
Pidy
Nice insidy
Apple pie.

B was once a little bear,
Beary
Wary
Hairy
Beary
Taky cary
Little bear.

B

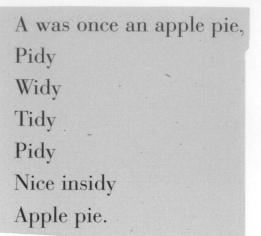

C was once a little cake,
Caky
Baky
Maky
Caky
Taky caky
Little cake.

D

D was once a little doll,
Dolly
Molly
Polly
Nolly
Nursy dolly
Little doll.

E

E was once a little eel,
Eely
Weely
Peely
Eely
Twirly tweely
Little eel.

F

F was once a little fish,
Fishy
Wishy
Squishy
Fishy
In a dishy
Little fish.

G was once a little goose,
Goosy
Moosy
Boosey
Goosey
Waddly woosy
Little goose.

G

H

H was once a little hen,
Henny
Chenny
Tenny
Henny
Eggsy any
Little hen.

I was once a bottle of ink,
Inky
Dinky
Thinky
Inky
Blacky minky
Bottle of ink.

J was once a jar of jam,
Jammy
Mammy
Clammy
Jammy
Sweety swammy
Jar of jam.

K

K was once a little kite,
Kity
Whity
Flighty
Kity
Out of sighty
Little kite.

L

L was once a little lark,
Larky
Marky
Harky
Larky
In the parky
Little lark.

M was once a little mouse,
Mousey
Bousey
Sousy
Mousy
In the housy
Little mouse.

N was once a little needle,
Needly
Tweedly
Threedly
Needly
Wisky wheedly
Little needle.

O was once a little owl,
Owly
Prowly
Howly
Owly
Browny fowly
Little owl.

P was once a little pump,
Pumpy
Slumpy
Flumpy
Pumpy
Dumpy thumpy
Little pump.

P

Q was once a little quail,
Quaily
Faily
Daily
Quaily
Stumpy taily
Little quail.

Q

R was once a little rose,
Rosy
Posy
Nosy
Rosy
Blows-y grows-y
Little rose.

S

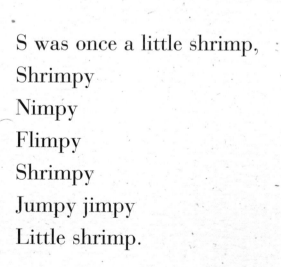

S was once a little shrimp,
Shrimpy
Nimpy
Flimpy
Shrimpy
Jumpy jimpy
Little shrimp.

T

T was once a little thrush,
Thrushy
Hushy
Bushy
Thrushy
Flitty flushy
Little thrush.

U

U was once a little urn,
Urny
Burny
Turny
Urny
Bubbly burny
Little urn.

V was once a little vine,
Viny
Winy
Twiny
Viny
Twisty twiny
Little vine.

V

The Great Whale of Wales

W

W was once a whale,
Whaly
Scaly
Shaly
Whaly
Tumbly taily
Mighty whale.

X

X was once a great king Xerxes,
Xerxy
Perxy
Turxy
Xerxy
Linxy Lurxy
Great King Xerxes.

Y

Y was once a little Yew,
Yewdy
Fewdy
Crudy
Yewdy
Growdy grewdy
Little yew.

Z was once a piece of zinc,
Tinky
Winky
Blinky
Tinky
Tinkly minky
Piece of zinc.